Cat Wishes

Words by Calista Brill

pictures by Kenard Pak

HOUGHTON MIFFLIN HARCOURT

Boston   New York

Once in the windy wood, there was a hungry Cat.

"A mouse, a mole, a bat," Cat said.

"I wish I had something to eat."

Rustle

Crouch,

coil,

pounce!

Cat caught a wiggly snake.

"Spare my life," the snake told Cat. "I'll grant you what you wish."

"No such thing as a wish," Cat said. His whiskers danced.

"Sure of that, are you?" said Snake.

Cat flicked his ears. "Maybe I'm not so hungry after all."

He lifted his paw.

"Three wishes for you!" said Snake.

He wiggled off through the grass.

"No such thing as a wish,"
Cat said. His belly growled.
"But if there were, I'd wish for a fish."

Pad,

   pad,

    pad,

Cat walked on
whisper feet.

Pad,

pad,

splash!

Cat stared with
wide cat eyes.

"No such thing as a wish," Cat said.

Burp.

Cat circled and circled and circled once more.

It was time to nap in the sun.

But the breezy air turned cold and damp,
and rain began to fall.

"No such thing as a wish," Cat said.
His tail lashed. "But if there were,
I'd wish for a house."

Plop,

plop,

plop,

the rain spotted Cat's fur.

Plop,

plop,

plop,

Cat's nose tickled and twitched.

Sniff!

Cat smelled a roasty, toasty fireplace.

Cat saw a winking light.

Cat walked into his very own house
and curled up on a cushion.

"No such thing as a wish," Cat said.

Cat woke up in the night
surrounded by shadows.

"No such thing as a wish," Cat said.

"But if there were, I'd wish for a friend."

Shuff,

shuff,

shuff

came a footstep. Cat's tail bristled.

"Hello!"
A very small girl stood at the door.

"A wiggly snake in the windy
woods granted me three wishes,"
the small girl said.

"First I was hungry."
Cat saw her picnic basket.

"And then it was raining."
Cat saw her red raincoat.

"And then I was lonely."
Cat climbed into her arms.

Prrr_

To my mom and dad —C.B.

For Kate, I'm ever so grateful —K.P.

Library of Congress Cataloging-in-Publication Data
Names: Brill, Calista, author. | Pak, Kenard, illustrator.
Title: Cat wishes / by Calista Brill ; illustrated by Kenard Pak.
Description: Boston ; New York : Houghton Mifflin Harcourt, [2018] | Summary:
"A cat who professes not to believe in wishes is granted three of them,
but makes them nonetheless."—Provided by publisher.
Identifiers: LCCN 2016032910 | ISBN 9780544610552 (hardcover)
Subjects: | CYAC: Cats—Fiction. | Wishes—Fiction.
Classification: LCC PZ7.1.B755 Cat 2018 | DDC [E]—dc23
LC record available at https://lccn.loc.gov/2016032910

Manufactured in China
SCP 10 9 8 7 6 5 4 3 2 1
4500707516